This Little Tiger book belongs to:

_____

_____

_____

For Jeanette, George and Iris
– J C

LITTLE TIGER PRESS LTD.
an imprint of the Little Tiger Group
1 Coda Studios, 189 Munster Road,
London SW6 6AW
www.littletiger.co.uk

First published in Great Britain 2007
This edition published 2017

Ted, Bo and Diz

The First Adventure

Jason Chapman

LITTLE TIGER

LONDON

It was a warm, sunny morning.
Ted, Bo and Diz were at the beach.

"It's a lovely day . . ." sang Ted as
he pumped up the raft.
   ". . . to be by the ocean!" sang Diz,
shaking out the towels.

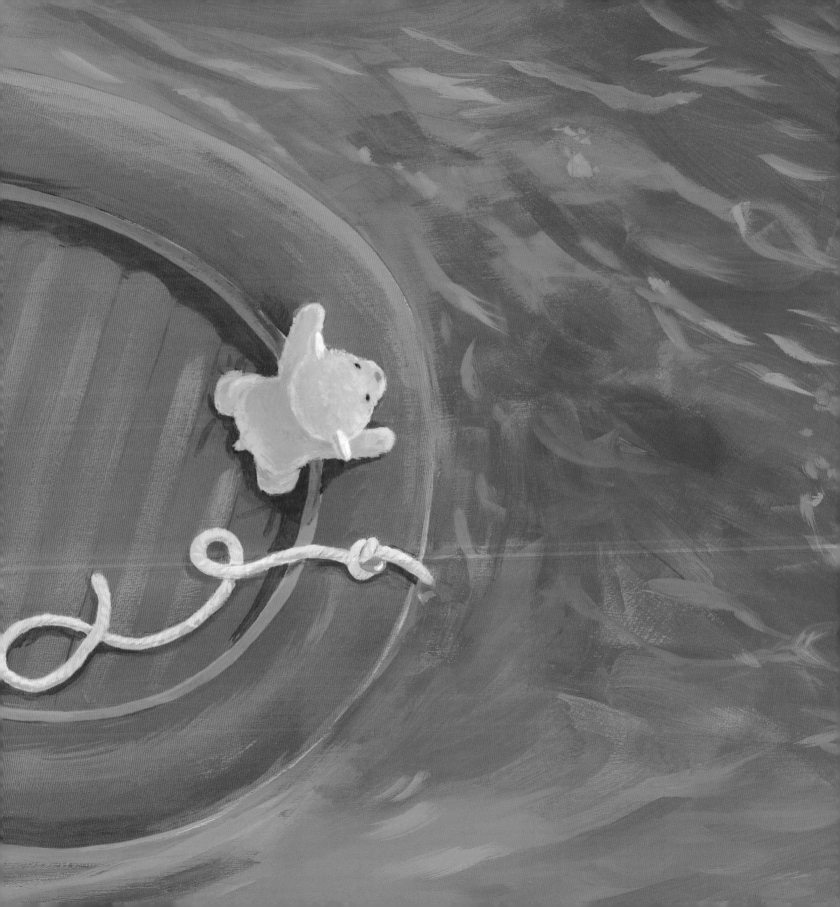

"Look," hollered Diz. "Is that an iceberg?"

There, all curled up on the softly rocking bed of ice,
lay a family of polar bears and a baby seal.

One by one, they woke up.

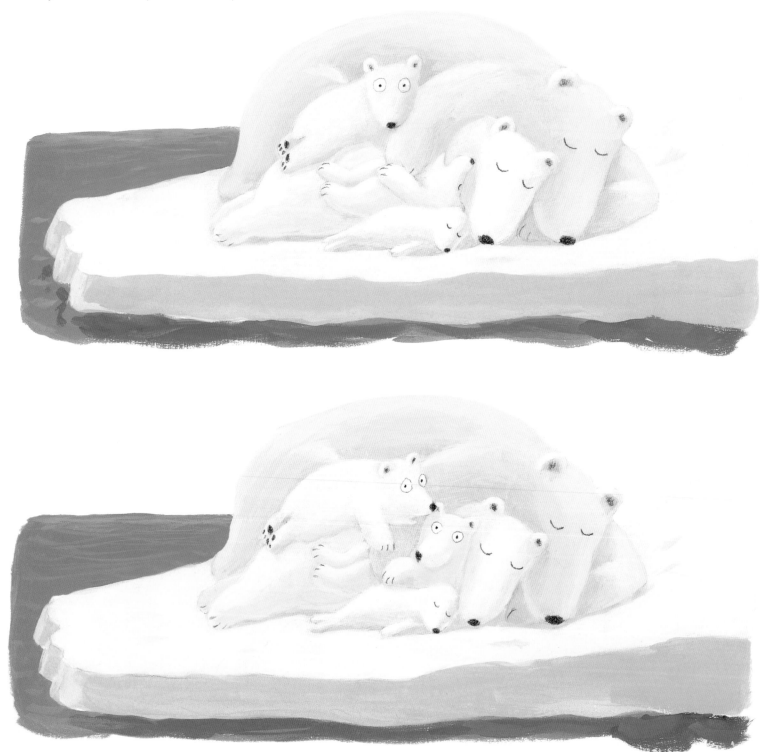

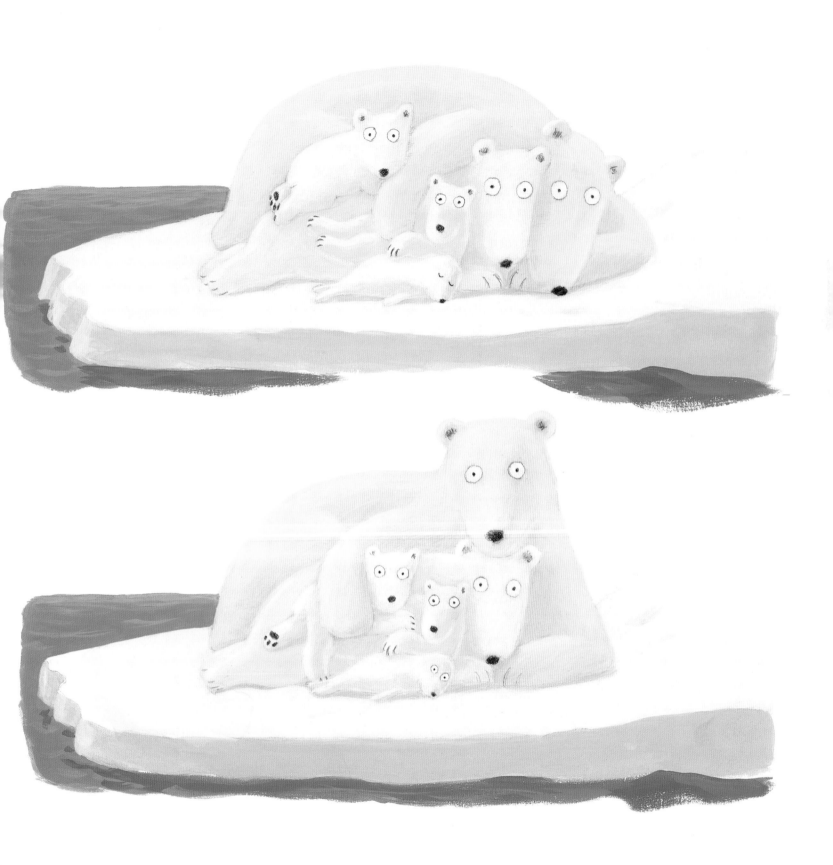

Ted, Bo and Diz paddled gently towards them.
As Bo leaned forward to give the smallest
polar bear a flower, she felt the coolness of
the icy boat on her face.

The little bear had never seen a flower before,
but he knew it was beautiful.

Under the warm sun the bears told stories of their icy world. The new friends played together, making snow castles on their island of ice.

Suddenly there was a dull crack.
The ice beneath Diz's feet broke off
and slipped away.
  "JUMP!" they all shouted.
  Diz jumped high and long, landing
safely with his friends . . .

Their island was melting!
"We could paddle home
in the boat," said
Daddy Polar Bear, but
it was too small for
all of them.

They sat and they
thought. And as they
thought, their
island got smaller . . .

and smaller.

Suddenly Ted jumped
into the boat.
"Wait here!" he said.
"I've got an idea."

"Be careful, Ted!" called Bo.
The new friends huddled together as
they watched Ted paddle far out to sea.

"Ted's coming back," said Daddy Polar Bear.
"He's coming back very fast!" said Diz.
Ted was with a family of whales!
"Hop aboard," said the biggest whale.

Ted, Bo and Diz waved goodbye as the bears and
baby seal set off on their long journey home.
   Soon the iceberg was no bigger than a pebble
on the beach. Bo picked it up and held it until
there was nothing left.

"Let's go home," said Ted sadly.
Diz looked out to sea and smiled.

"Look," he said. "Another iceberg!"